Cubby's Very Grumpy Day

By Maria Maysen

Illustrated by
Kasia Nowowiejska

SCHOLASTIC INC.

For Desmond and Wren
—M.M.

For my little Helenka—can't wait to meet you
—K.N.

10 9 8 7 6 5 4 3 2   17 18 19 20 21

ISBN 978-1-338-03817-0

Printed in the U.S.A.   40
First printing 2017

Artwork by Kasia Nowowiejska / Good Illustration Ltd.

Book design by Jennifer Rinaldi

"Good morning, Cubby! Time to wake up for school,"
calls Cubby's mommy.

Cubby groans. He is still sleepy!

"I'm having a bad day and the day hasn't even started yet!" says Cubby.

"Cheer up, Cubby!" says his mommy. "Daddy made you oatmeal for breakfast."

Cubby is grumpy through breakfast. "My oatmeal is too lumpy," he says.

"Cheer up, Cubby!" says Cubby's daddy. "Remember, today your class is taking a field trip to the museum."

"Oh yeah!" Cubby perks up a little bit. "Monkey and I are going to be seat buddies on the bus!"

But when Cubby gets to school, his day gets even worse. "I'm sorry, class, but our trip to the museum has been postponed until tomorrow," says Ms. Elephant.

"Oh no!" says the class.

"OH NO!" says Cubby.

"Cheer up, Cubby!" says Monkey. "We can be seat buddies at lunch!"
"Okay," Cubby sighs. He tries to feel better.

But at lunch, Cubby discovers his mom accidentally gave him *her* lunch: stewed beans and tomatoes — the yuckiest lunch ever.

"Oh yuck!" says Cubby.

"Cheer up . . ." Zebra starts to say.

"I DON'T WANT TO CHEER UP!" Cubby shouts.

"Cubby, is everything all right?" asks Ms. Elephant.

"I'm having a bad day!" says Cubby, sniffing.

"And he DOES NOT want to cheer up," says Monkey.

"Do you want to tell us about it?" asks Ms. Elephant.

"I COULDN'T SLEEP LAST NIGHT AND MY OATMEAL WAS LUMPY AND OUR TRIP GOT CANCELED AND MOMMY PACKED THE WRONG LUNCH FOR ME!" Cubby wails.

"That does sound like a bad day," says Ms. Elephant.

"The worst," agrees Monkey.

"When I have a bad day, I like to run until my spots blur," says Cheetah.

"When I have a bad day, I count my stripes and it makes me feel better," says Zebra.

"And I like to hang by my tail when I have a bad day!" says Monkey. "Everything looks better upside down. You should try it!"

"But I don't have spots to blur or stripes to count or a strong monkey tail to hang from," says Cubby miserably.

"Hmm," says Monkey. "I have an idea!"

"WHEEEEE!" yells Cubby.

"Forty-one, forty-two, forty-three . . . Wow! Forty-three stripes!" counts Cubby.

"Everything DOES look better upside down!"
laughs Cubby.

"Cubby, it looks like your bad day got better!" says Ms. Elephant after lunch. "Was it because you talked about what was bothering you?"

"Or was it because you zoomed really fast?" asks Cheetah.

"Or because you counted
forty-three stripes?" asks Zebra.

"Or because you were upside
down?" asks Monkey.

Cubby smiles. "All of those things did help a little. But that wasn't what made me feel better. What made me feel better was . . .

. . . doing all of those things with you!"